LOVE & LESSONS WHEN I WAS SEVENTEEN

SHRUTI KARALE

For those who loved deeply, fell, and found the strength to
get back up.
For the hearts that broke but healed with every lesson love
brought.
This story is for those who kept believing in love, even
when it seemed hard.

And to my younger self, who thought every goodbye was
the end—thank you for showing me that some goodbyes
are just new beginnings.

Contents

Preface

Love in our teenage years is like stepping into a world filled
with excitement, dreams, and confusion. It's a time when
every emotion feels intense, every moment feels like
forever, and every goodbye feels like the end. Yet, it's also a
time when we learn some of the most important
lessons—about love, life, and ourselves.
This story isn't just about the highs of young love or
the heartache that often follows. It's about the
journey—learning to grow through the struggles, the
mistakes, and the moments of joy. It's about finding
strength in vulnerability and realizing that sometimes, the
hardest lessons are the ones that shape us the most.
As you read, I hope you see parts of your own story
reflected in these pages
Thank you for picking up this book. I hope you enjoy
the journey as much as I've enjoyed writing it
Happy reading !!!

Acknowledgements

Writing this novel has been a journey filled with challenges and growth, taking me nearly ten months to finish this story. There were countless times when I felt like giving up, but during those moments, my online friends provided the support I needed to keep going.

I also want to thank my elder brother for always asking, "Kitna likh liye?" Your encouragement and belief in me made a significant difference. Without your support, I might never have completed this book.

Thank you all for being part of this journey and for always being there.

1

where it all started

I was in that same old room, deep in contemplation, wondering if I'd ever accomplish anything significant in my life...I wasn't exactly a top student - more like an average overthinker and a complete disaster when it came to math, my parents had a special talent of disliking my friends and, quite frankly they couldn't stand by my company either. so when my 10th grade marks landed they decided to send me off to boarding school...and I was thrilled - just kidding, I was not it felt like punishment, but over time I figured a new environment might help me grow.... My friends who are significantly better and some even above 90% seem to have it all together, whenever I call them for advice and ask them about their studies, their responses were casually dismissive:

"Oh Maria, I haven't even started yet!

It was a harsh realization that my mom had been right about my friends- they were all pretending to be something they weren't. this wasn't about comparing the grades; it was about recognizing that friends who lie about their studies aren't the kind of people you can rely on. I needed friends I could trust.

It was a period in my life when I felt a mix of happiness and nervousness. The prospect of experiencing a new environment brought me excitement and a sense of anticipation. At the same time, I was quite anxious because I had never been alone before, and I questioned whether I would be able to handle being so far from home. The thought of managing everything on my own was daunting.

I chose the commerce stream for my 11th and 12th grades.Before the school year officially began, we had a month of online classes....During this time, I not only performed well academically but also managed to forge some meaningful friendships. This initial period of adjustment was both challenging and rewarding, setting the stage for my journey ahead.

I was so sure I wouldn't get caught up in any boyfriend-girlfriend drama and would just focus on studying. But life must have found that thought hilarious because, well, what's meant to happen, just happens—whether you want it or not.

I had arrived at the hostel a day ahead of schedule, eager to set up my room and prepare myself for the classes that would begin the following day. My excitement wasn't just about getting settled in; it was also about meeting my new online friends in person for the first time. One of them, vivan, was particularly special. We were classmates and had online classes together for 1 ½ months. And before we knew it, we started talking so much, even during online classes. I was so excited to finally meet him in real life." before we arrived for offline class and he had been studying at the same school since nursery he was day boarder and I was hosteler as you all know and, and over time, we had had build string bond despite never having met face-to-face.

So, when the moment finally arrived and I stepped into the classroom, I was brimming with anticipation what I did not realize was that Vivan was already there, seated among the students, as I entered the room, my eyes scanned the space eagerly. When I spotted him, my excitement was so overwhelming, I was haste to reach him, I stumbled over my desk and nearly lost my balance. It was a classic case of enthusiasm gone away, where my grand entrance turned into a rather clumsy spectacle. But in that moment, my joy at seeing vivan far outweighed my lack of grace. That was my unforgettable first impression - an exuberant mix of joy and awkwardness

It felt like love at first sight for me, though I had already resolved not to pursue any kind of relationship. Still, there was no denying that I felt a certain magnetic attraction towards him

If I were to describe him, it would be impossible not to start with his smile - it was, without exaggeration, the best smile in the world. There was something utterly captivating about it, a blend of warmth and charm that seemed to light up the room. His physique was equally impressive he had a presence that commanded attention. His jawline was striking, complementing attention. A perfectly groomed beard that added to his allure. His hair, tousled just enough to look effortlessly stylish framed his face in a way that was almost poetic.

The veins in his hand seemed to underscore his physical vitality, and his voice- smooth and confident- had a way of drawing you in, making you want to listen to his speak for hours. Everything about his seemed to be in perfect harmony, a blend of attributes that made him seem almost too good to be true.But he wasn't just a pretty face. He was exceptionally talented, excelling both in sports and academics, his achievement in these areas only added to his impressive persona, making him someone who is not only admirable but genuinely remarkable. Despite my decision to stay away from any romantic entanglements, there was no escaping the fact that he had captured my attention in a way that was both profound and undeniable.

And then, he walked over to me, and we shared our first handshake.

Hey are you okay ?he asked

I said, "Yeah, I'm fine," and our eye contact—it was something special, like the beginning of a connection between us.

I can hardly describe it. The magic of that moment. As our hands met, it felt as though time itself had slowed down, and the world around us simply act of shaking hands became something extraordinary.

The touch was electrifying, sending a rush of sensations through me. It was as if has hand had a warmth and firmness that conveyed a connection far deeper a connection far deeper than a mere greeting. I could almost feel the spark of energy travelling from his hand to mine, creating a fluttering sensation in my stomach that was both exhilarating and comforting

The first touch of his hand was not just a handshake it was a magical encounter that made everything feel more vibrant and full of promise.

2

Meet the crew

My hostel life would have been nothing without my friends—honestly, without them, it would have been incredibly boring. Each one of them is so unique, with such distinct personalities. They were everything to me in the hostel—my parents, siblings, my entire world.4 of us me, Prerna, chavi and somya

Prerna- the epitome of intelligence and wisdom.always buzzing with ideas, and she has an uncanny ability to grasp even the most complex concepts with ease. But beyond her brilliance, she possesses a warmth that makes her approachable.

Chavi - on the other hand, is the life of the party. She's the kind of person who can turn even the most mundane situation into something hilarious. Her sense of humor is infectious, and she's always ready with a witty remark or a funny story..And whenever I would zone out in class from overthinking, Chavi would keep hitting my hand, saying, maira class maira class....

Somya- was actually one of the most carefree and daring individuals in the group. She lives life on her own terms, unbothered by what others think or say. Her strength lies in her ability to stay true to herself, regardless of the circumstances.

And wait,

No way I can forget Shweta.

Since starting boarding school in the 9th grade, Shweta has become an expert in hostel life. Her experience has made her a strong, resilient, and loyal friend. She quickly becomes one of my closest allies, and her formidable reputation ensures that no one dares to cross me. Anyone who tries to trouble me knows they'll have to face Shweta. However, Shweta had a deep-seated dislike for Vivan. From the moment I mentioned that I liked him more than just a friend, she constantly warned me that he wasn't right for me. Despite her warnings, I never sensed anything negative about Vivan, so I figured Shweta simply didn't like him.

It's funny how life brings people together, binding them in ways they never expected. We were a group that spent every waking moment together, from the moment we dragged ourselves out of bed in the morning to the time we finally crashed at night. It wasn't always sunshine and rainbows; in fact, there were days when we'd drive each other crazy, with the smallest habits grating on our nerves. Someone would forget to clean up, someone else would play music too loud, and let's not even talk about the fights over who got to use the bathroom first.

But despite all the little annoyances, we couldn't stand to be apart. It was as if the universe had stitched us together, creating an unspoken bond that even the worst arguments couldn't break. We knew each other's quirks, our highs and lows, our strengths and weaknesses, and somehow, that made the chaos of being together worth it.

Sometimes, in the middle of all the bickering and frustrations, there'd be this quiet moment of realization.

We'd look around and just know—no matter how much we might irritate each other, life without this madness, without these people, would be empty. We were like a mismatched puzzle that somehow fit perfectly together. And even on the days when we felt like we needed a break from one another, the truth was, we couldn't really imagine being without each other.

So, we kept going, navigating through the ups and downs, knowing that the bonds we shared were stronger than the temporary annoyances. After all, it wasn't just about living under the same hostel; it was about building memories that would last a lifetime, memories that we knew we'd cherish even when the days of living together were long gone.

3
The art of silent conversation

In my school, the idea of girls and boys talking to each other was treated with the same seriousness as a national security threat. It was as if the moment a boy and girl exchanged words, the fabric of the universe would unravel. The rules were ironclad: girls on one side, boys on the other, and never the twain shall meet. The teachers made it their life's mission to enforce this separation, and they did it with the zeal of secret agents guarding state secrets.

Being a hostler added another layer to this already complex equation. We didn't have the luxury of mobile phones like the day scholars. No, our connection to the outside world was restricted to a single 30-minute window once a week. For that half-hour, the world stopped, and all of us hostlers would line up to make our calls home, like soldiers on leave. It was the only time we could hear the voices of our families, get updates from the outside world, and remind ourselves that there was life beyond the four walls of our school.

But for me, those 30 minutes had a different purpose as

well. You see, I had memorized Vivan's number long ago. It wasn't enough to just see him in class, exchanging glances across the room. Our teachers were like walking CCTV cameras, constantly monitoring us, ensuring that not a word was spoken between boys and girls. A simple "hi" could earn you a scolding, and a longer conversation? That was out of the question.

So, when I got my precious 30 minutes with the phone, I had to be strategic. I spent the first 15 minutes talking to my parents, telling them everything was fine, school was good, I was studying hard— all the things they wanted to hear. But the last 15 minutes, those were mine. I'd quickly dial Vivan's number, heart pounding, praying the line would connect. And when it did, we had to make every second count.

It was Sunday and we got our phones

And this was the first conversation of me and vivan on call after reaching school. I deal his number immediately after taking at home.

Hey! I can't believe you picked up so quickly. Were you just waiting by the phone? I asked

Hey! Well, maybe just a little. I've been hoping you'd call. It feels like forever since we last talked. He replied

Me- I know, right? It's so different now. I still remember the first time I saw you in class. I was so nervous I practically fell over when I saw you.

Vivian- Oh, I remember. You were like a cartoon character, tripping over your own feet and trying to play it cool. It was pretty hilarious...hahahahah!!

Me- Thanks for the reminder! now will you stop laughing on me.

Vivian - okayyy sorry sorry hahahaha...

Me- vivannnnnn

vivan - yeah done! maira I miss those moments we had before school started. We used to talk for hours, and now it feels like we barely have a moment.

Me- I miss those conversations too. It was nice just being able to talk freely. It's hard to adjust to not having that anymore.

Vivian - Definitely. I keep thinking about how nice it would be to have a real conversation again, not just these short calls.

Me - I feel the same way. But I've only got 15 minutes before the warden starts giving me the stare of doom.

Vivan - Ah, the infamous stare. I remember it well. Better not keep her waiting!

Me- Definitely not. I'll be in trouble if she catches me talking on the phone more than the time. It's like she has a sixth sense for these things.

Vivan- Haha, I believe it. Well, I guess we'll have to make the most of these short calls then.

Me- Absolutely. I'm really glad we can still talk, even if it's brief. It means a lot to me.

Ok ok bye ma'am is coming see you tomorrow vivan bye

As soon as he even said bye I had to cut the call and submit it to the warden.

We talked about everything and nothing, laughing at the absurdity of our situation. We knew that once those 15 minutes were up, we'd be back to silent glances and secret smiles, trying to communicate in a school where words between us were forbidden.

In those moments, we became experts in the art of silent communication. We mastered the subtle glance, the quick nod, the shared smile that spoke volumes without a word. Our teachers might have acted like CCTV, but they couldn't catch the invisible conversations that passed between us.

Those 15 minutes each week were our lifeline, a connection that the strictest rules couldn't sever.

So yes, school was strict, and talking to Vivan was a challenge. But it was a challenge we both took on with a smile, knowing that some connections can't be silenced, no matter how hard the world tries.

4

Happiness and Heartache

The school day commenced promptly at 7:30 a.m., and the hostel imposed a strict curfew of 6:45 a.m. for us to be out of the building. Missing this deadline meant facing the warden's ire, a consequence none of us wanted to endure. Despite the early hour and the chill that nipped at my skin, I never wavered from my routine. My unwavering punctuality was driven by a singular, compelling motivation: catching a glimpse of Vivan. The anticipation of seeing him each morning gave me a reason to embrace the early start and the cold, knowing that the reward would be worth every sacrifice.

This particular morning followed the familiar pattern. I hurried to the benches that lined the pathway outside our classroom, my breath forming small clouds in the crisp air. The school bus, with its predictable delays, was a mere backdrop to the real event I awaited with bated breath. My eyes were fixed on the sand-covered path, the same route Vivan always took. As I waited, my heart quickened with every passing minute, eager for the sight that would make the morning complete. Finally, as he appeared, dressed in his impeccably fitted school uniform and carrying his green bag, it felt as though time had stretched and slowed just for this moment. He seemed to glide into view, every detail enhanced by the slow-motion effect of my infatuation—the gentle sway of his uniform, the playful dance of the breeze through his hair, and the fleeting yet meaningful exchange of our gazes. It was a scene straight out of a romantic film, where every element came together to create a perfect, almost cinematic, moment.

Reflecting on it all, it's almost comical how breakfast became a secondary concern. Each day, I willingly sacrificed my morning meal just to witness that brief, magical encounter. The irony was not lost on me: I was exchanging the comfort of a fresh and hot breakfast for a fleeting glimpse of Vivan, finding a strange satisfaction in the absurdity of my devotion. The sight of him walking towards me, the fleeting connection we shared in those moments, made missing breakfast seem not only acceptable but entirely worth it.

It was supposed to be one of those perfect mornings when everything seemed to fall into place. Vivan arrived with his usual effortless grace, and as our eyes met, we shared a smile that spoke volumes—a silent conversation that had become the highlight of my day. We turned toward our respective classes, our hearts light and hopeful, buoyed by the joy of seeing each other.

But then, as we reached the notice board, a cold wave of reality crashed over us. A page detailing the section divisions had been pinned up. My heart dropped as I saw Vivan's name listed under Section 1. Desperately, I searched for my own name, my fingers trembling with a mix of fear and hope. The cruel truth was soon undeniable—our sections had been split.

It felt as though the ground had given way beneath my feet. I could feel the tears brimming in my eyes, but I fought them back with every ounce of strength I had. We exchanged one final, heart-wrenching glance, our smiles now a painful memory. The shared moments of quiet conversations and meaningful glances in the same class were gone, and with them, a part of me seemed to crumble. Prerna and Shweta were in Section A with Vivan, while Chavi and Somya were with me in Section B. The reality of facing this new day without Vivan's comforting presence was almost unbearable. It was as if the fragile bubble of happiness we had built around ourselves had burst, leaving us to confront the harsh truth of our separation. The world suddenly felt colder, and the morning that had begun with such promise ended in a deep, sorrowful void.

And after that two long months of school, Diwali holidays were finally here. I was bursting with excitement—not just to see my family, but also because I could finally talk to Vivan as much as I wanted. Ten whole days of freedom stretched ahead, and I couldn't wait to fill them with conversations and moments I had missed.

Papa had booked my bus ticket, and that morning, we were given back our phones—small but significant keys to the world we had left behind. I had a simple keypad phone, but the thought of home and Vivan kept me company. The journey seemed to fly by, and before I knew it, I was almost home. The hours melted away.

Arriving home, I savored the taste of home-cooked food and spent the evening catching up with family. But the moment I had been waiting for all day was still ahead. As night fell, I picked up my phone and called Vivan. We talked for two blissful hours, our words flowing easily as if no time had passed. It felt perfect, but a part of me hesitated to express how deeply I cared for him. I feared that if he didn't feel the same, I could lose not just him but also our cherished friendship. So, I kept my feelings hidden, buried under layers of doubt and hesitation.

Then, one night, I casually mentioned another guy to him, just sharing a random story. His reaction spoke volumes. Though he didn't say much, his tone revealed something I hadn't expected. He seemed possessive, and in that moment, I realized—maybe, just maybe, he felt the same way about me. Our friendship was more than just that for him too.

At school, I had told Vivan about the endless proposals I received over the last two months. When he asked if I liked any of them, I said no, not really. And then, out of nowhere, he said, "I love you." The world seemed to stop. I couldn't believe what I had just heard. "What did you say?" I asked, needing to hear it again.

"I love you, Maira," he repeated. "I don't know if you feel the same, but I couldn't keep it to myself any longer. I was afraid to tell you, afraid you might not feel the same way. But now, seeing so many guys interested in you, I realized I might lose you if I don't say it. I love you, Maira."

For a moment, I was silent, letting his words sink in. Then, overwhelmed with joy, I confessed, "I love you too, Vivan! I was so scared of losing you if I confessed, but I've felt the same way all along."

Our love was sealed with joy and laughter as we repeatedly said "I love you" to each other, marveling at how we had both been holding back the same feelings. That night, everything changed. Our friendship, already precious, transformed into something deeper.

Later, our usual late-night conversation turned to past relationships. We both shared our past relationships with each other and it was all good, until I saw her name on Instagram. To my shock, Vedika was at a Diwali party with Vivan. He had told me they didn't talk anymore, but there she was, smiling beside him.

That night, I confronted Vivan. "Did you meet your ex?" I asked, trying to keep my voice steady. "I saw the story on Instagram."

There was a pause. "Yeah, I did," he admitted. "But I didn't know she was going to be there."

"Didn't you ask who was coming?" I couldn't hide my hurt.

"I did, but my friends didn't tell me. I swear it wasn't intentional," he said, his voice softening.

"Really?" I questioned, struggling to trust.

"Maira, don't you trust me?" he pleaded.

"I do, I do," I whispered, more to convince myself.

"I'm sorry," he said earnestly. "I didn't mean to hurt you. It won't happen again."

tried to shake off the unease, but doubt lingered. It was the first time Vivan had hurt me, and I couldn't ignore the heaviness in my chest. Love, even the deepest kind, comes with its uncertainties. Seeing him with his ex was a blow, but I didn't want to make a big deal out of it. I knew it wasn't entirely his fault, and I needed to find a way to move past it.

So, after that night, everything was back to normal between us. But for some reason, I found myself missing my annoying friends from school. Like, of course I'd remember them since we spent every single day together. I missed nagging Chavi to clean the bed, struggling with accounts with Prerna, and endlessly sharing everything with Somya. It's funny how I missed all those little things. But hey, at least I got to hang out with my family. Honestly, leaving home made me realize how much life has changed. Now I have to handle everything myself—no more mom around to solve every problem!

5

Narrow escape

So, after wrapping up my wonderful holiday with family, it was time to head back to the hostel. And let me tell you, leaving the comfort of home is never easy. I packed up all the love and warmth that came with mom's food. but in the end, I had no choice but to hop on the bus and head back to the hostel. The comfort of home? Well, that stayed behind.

Six hours later, I arrived at the hostel. My roommates hadn't arrived yet, so there I was, alone in the room. The silence felt heavy, and all I could think about was home. The longing hit harder than I expected. But you know, that's life, isn't it? To move forward, you've got to leave something behind. Comfort comes with a price. I kept telling myself that as I started organizing my almirah, trying to distract myself. Took a bath, trying to wash away the homesickness. And then, just like magic, my crazy friends arrived. And with them? No more sad Vibes, just pure fun!

The next day, I found myself waiting for Vivan. I was sitting on the bench outside the classroom, glancing at the entrance every few minutes. And then, there he was, walking towards me from the sandy side of the ground. But this time, something felt different. This time, he wasn't just

Vivan, my friend—he was Vivan, my boyfriend. I blush like a tomato the moment our eyes meet! Trying to keep things low-key, we quickly shook hands, hoping no one would notice. That little handshake was all I needed. It made my whole day. I think I was blushing all the way through class after that.

I remember one particular day when Vivan didn't show up to school. I waited for him, but when he didn't arrive, I had to ask one of his friends what was going on. "He's not feeling well," his friend said. "He won't be coming for the next two days." And just like that, I was stressed out of my mind. No calls, no texts—nothing. The thing is, our relationship was a secret from Vivan's friends, and he insisted on keeping it that way so word wouldn't spread around the school.

Later that day, our accounts teacher was looking for Vivan to get some work done. He and Chavi were sitting on the bench outside the class, solving some questions. Out of nowhere, the teacher asked Chavi to grab his register because he needed Vivan's number. And what does my lovely, brilliant Chavi do? Instead of getting the register, she shouts, "Hey Maira! You probably know Vivan's number, right? Just tell me!"

She realized what she had said the moment the words left her mouth. And me? Like a complete idiot, I rushed over and rattled off Vivan's number as if I'd been waiting for this moment my whole life. It wasn't until I finished giving the last digit that it hit me—what in the world did I just do? I was done for.

That day, my teacher called me aside for a private talk. "What's going on between you and Vivan?" he asked, his tone serious. And just like that, things had gotten way too real. I didn't want to drag Vivan into this mess, so I looked him straight in the eye and said, "Sir, Vivan's a good friend of mine. My parents even know about him, and they think highly of him."

The teacher paused for a moment before replying, "I'll talk to your parents tomorrow, then."

Panic hit me like a truck. I didn't have my phone with me, so how was I supposed to explain the situation to my parents before the teacher talked to them? I ended up writing a letter. The warden's daughter, who had become a good friend of mine, agreed to help, and she passed the letter on to my mom. In it, I explained everything—every detail. Luckily, my mom understood the situation and handled it before it could blow up into a disaster. Thank goodness for cool mom

That next Sunday, my mom, dad, and I had a long conversation—one of those talks where you lay everything on the table. And honestly, it felt good to have it all out in the open.

6

The note

Our school was like a fortress against modern technology—no internet, no phones, and iPads strictly controlled after school hours. By this time, Vivan and I had been separated into different classes, but nothing could break our connection. We found clever ways to stay in touch, no matter the restrictions. We used the Notes app on our iPads to write to each other—our own little secret in a place that didn't want us to communicate. Whenever a break came, I'd rush over to his class.and quickly take photos of each other's notes, and save them. With AirDrop disabled on our devices, this was our only way to stay connected. And then on Sunday we discuss everything in that 15 min call where we'd talk about everything we couldn't share during the week. Sometimes, we even wrote each other handwritten letters, slipping them into our bags when no one was looking.

One day, things almost went horribly wrong. I was lost in writing another note, completely absorbed in my thoughts. It felt like just another ordinary day. But something was off, something lurking just out of sight. One of the staff, assigned to watch over us during evening study sessions, was quietly creeping up on me. These staff were there to ensure we were actually studying, not wasting time. Among them was one we called "the Witch." She seemed to have it out for commerce girls, always finding a reason to hover near us, as if waiting for the perfect moment to catch us doing something wrong.

That day, she thought she had finally caught me. There I was, lost in writing, hiding the letter in my notebook as I always did. My friends knew I often wrote letters to Vivan, and they always looked out for me. Prerna was the first to see the Witch slowly approaching. Her heart probably skipped a beat, and in a desperate attempt to save me, she shouted, "maira, give me your accounts book!" The urgency in her voice snapped me out of my trance, but it was too late. The Witch's hand darted forward and snatched the letter right out of my hands. My friends froze, their breaths caught in their throats, as if the world had stopped. My heart was pounding—I was certain I was doomed. This was it. I was sure they'd expel me on the spot

But then, everything took an unexpected turn. You see, this time, I wasn't writing to Vivan. No secret love note, no hidden words meant just for him. This time, I was writing to one of my juniors. The board exams were coming up, and I had grown close to some of them. And after a few months we'll be leaving school so I was just writing them that I love them and I'll always be there for him like there Older sister in and outside of school. So, while the Witch was eagerly anticipating the chance to finally get me expelled, her plan fell apart. Her dream of getting me thrown out of school? Just that—a dream. I could almost see the disappointment in her eyes when she realized her "big catch" was nothing more than a harmless letter of encouragement.

The truth is, she had dragged us to the principal's office many times before, always eager to catch us in the act—whether it was for sneaking movies or music onto our iPads, or just finding any excuse to scold us. But looking back, those moments turned into some of our best memories. Years from now, when we're all older and catching up over a call, we won't be reminiscing about solving accounts problems or memorizing business studies. No, we'll be laughing about how seven girls in commerce—especially the five of us—created the craziest, most unforgettable memories. We got scolded plenty, but we lived those moments to the fullest, making sure that even the Witch couldn't stop us from enjoying our time together.

7
The weight of Expectations

Birthdays. I don't know why, but I've always been incredibly excited about mine. Every single year, I plan every detail, from the dress to the celebration, imagining how perfect it would be. And for some reason, every single year, I end up crying. This time was no different. I had been thinking about my birthday for a whole month, reminding my friends daily, "Only 30 days left... now 20... now 10." But when the day finally arrived, something unexpected happened, something heart-breaking.

At school, regardless of the day, we were allowed to call home only under the warden's supervision. But this time, my birthday was on a Sunday. This meant I'd be able to call not just home, but Vivan too! I was so happy. That night, my dear friends had planned the sweetest surprise for me. I cut our classic biscuit cake, and to my surprise, I received a gift from a boy who secretly liked me. It was a watch. When I saw it, I realized it was expensive, too much for me to accept. I couldn't take it, so I returned it to the girl who had given it to me.

It was sweet of him, though—he had taken the risk of asking another girl to give it to me exactly at midnight. But I knew I couldn't keep it. I wrote a note, saying it was too expensive and that I appreciated the gesture, but I just couldn't accept it.

The next day, I woke up at 6 a.m., excitement buzzing inside me. I secretly took my iPad out from the iPad almirah and sneaked it into my room. iPads weren't allowed in the rooms, so I had to do it with a lot of patience and planning. We had even "misplaced" the keys to the warden's cupboard, where the iPads were kept, just to make sure she wouldn't lock them away. If she did, we wouldn't have gotten them until 9 a.m.—too late for what I needed. I eagerly turned on the router, connected to Instagram, and logged in quickly, ready to see Vivan's birthday wish.

He knew we used the internet on Sundays, and I was sure he'd send a message on Instagram, knowing I'd be online. But when I checked, there was nothing. No message from him. I thought, "Maybe he'll message later." But I kept checking, all the way till 12:30 p.m.—just an hour before our Sunday call. Still, nothing. I felt horrible. Everyone else had wished me, but not him. My heart felt heavy with disappointment.

I remembered his birthday, how even though it wasn't on a Sunday, we still managed to meet the next day in class. But I had made sure to wish him at midnight. I even went out of my way to get the warden's daughter involved, sneaking a card and Vivan's number to her, asking her to send him a message from her mom's phone. I was terrified the entire time, thinking, "What if the warden catches us?" But the next morning, when the warden's daughter told me the job was done, I felt relieved. Everything had gone smoothly, and Vivan received his message.

But today, despite Vivan having his phone with him, he hadn't bothered to send me a single message. It hurt so much.

Call time arrived, and first, I dialed home. My mom was at a function, and there was something wrong with her phone, so she didn't answer. I spoke to my dad for barely two minutes before the connection dropped due to bad reception. The frustration built up as I hung up, feeling like even my family wasn't there for me on my birthday.

Finally, I called Vivan. At this point, I was already frustrated. He picked up with so much excitement in his voice, "Happy Birthdayyy!" But all I could manage was a quiet, "Thank you." He noticed right away. "What happened?" he asked, his tone softening.

"Nothing," I replied, trying to hold back the tears.

"Come on, tell me," he pressed, even softer this time.

"You really don't know what happened?" I blurted out. "I've been waiting for your message all day, Vivan! Why didn't you text me? You had your phone, and I've been waiting since morning!"

I was upset, and my voice cracked as I tried to hold back the tears that were now impossible to stop. Everything had built up—the disappointment, the frustration with my family, and now Vivan's lack of effort.

He tried to apologize, but before he could finish, the call cut off. Time was up. I had to submit my phone. I went upstairs and cried. My friends tried to console me, but the hurt lingered.

Later that night, when I checked Instagram one last time, I saw it—Vivan's message. Two long paragraphs. He apologized, explaining that he should have known better and realized what I was expecting. His words were enough to make me forgive him.

But as I read his message, I couldn't help but reflect. Maybe birthdays are just like any other day. They bring these high expectations, and when things don't go exactly as we imagined, it hurts. Maybe birthdays shouldn't be taken so seriously. They just set us up for disappointment when reality doesn't match the fantasy we build in our heads....

8

Farewell to an almost goodbye

One week passed like a blur. Each day, I checked my Instagram, hoping for a message from Vivan. Each time, nothing. Not a single text. The void felt endless, and as the days stretched on, the silence weighed heavy on my heart. Not even picking up my call on Sunday It was Monday—the day of our farewell. The day I realized that my time in this hostel, in this classroom, with my stupid friends, and with Vivan, was slipping away faster than I could comprehend.

The day boarders were already gone, with study leave in full swing, and the hallways that used to echo with laughter and noise now felt quiet, abandoned. I missed waiting for him outside the class, the stolen glances during basketball games, skipping breakfast just to catch a glimpse of him. I missed the notes we'd sneakily exchange, the secret games of table tennis—despite me barely knowing how to play. I missed it all. That day, I decided something: if I met him, I'd speak to him properly. Maybe he didn't want to keep in contact after all. Maybe this was it. If it was, I'd say goodbye with grace, no matter how much it hurt.

Farewell day came. The boys were already gathered, trying to spot their girlfriends. The girls were doing the same, searching for their boyfriends. I arrived late, heart racing. And there he was—Vivan. Standing in the distance. Our eyes met, and time stood still. We just stared at each other, caught in the moment, while everything else faded into the background.

We didn't know what would happen next. We took our seats, but the weight of everything unsaid hung between us. Later, we met backstage. Without a word, he hugged me tight, and I could feel the pain of those five days melt away for just a moment.

"Where were you, stupid? I was so worried about you! You didn't care at all, did you?" I asked, my voice trembling, desperate for an explanation.

He looked at me, his eyes soft but apologetic. "My phone got stolen... I couldn't text you."

I wanted to believe him. I did. But something inside me still doubted it. Before I could say more, my friends called me for our dance performance. Me, a non-dancer, about to perform. I went anyway, lost in the whirlwind of emotions. But somehow, I danced my heart out. And it went better than I could have imagined.

After the performance, it was Vivan's turn to give a speech. Everyone was rushing to take pictures with their friends and partners. I was almost lost in the crowd, but when I saw him standing there, giving his speech, I had to listen. I moved closer.

His voice was steady, but his words hit deep: "Some relationships formed here are meant to end here... and some, to be taken forward."

As his speech ended, I was already walking away, trying to hold back my tears. But he caught up to me, pulling me aside. He leaned in close, whispered in my ear, "I'm sorry. And thank you."

His words hung in the air, and I could feel how genuine they were. He smiled, grateful that I had stayed to listen. And then, we took a photo together—our best photo ever. It captured a moment that I'll never forget.

Later, when I finally opened Instagram, there it was: a message from him. He explained everything. The reason he hadn't texted. His exams were approaching, and with his plans to pursue CA, he felt he couldn't balance both studies and our relationship. He thought ending things would be the right choice, for both of us.

Reading his words, I understood. I couldn't be angry. Instead, I told him, "It's your life, Vivan. If you think it won't work, then we won't force it. But I promise, I'll never stand in the way of your studies. I'll always understand."

He looked at me, eyes full of emotion, and said, "After seeing you stay to listen to my whole speech, even when everyone else was leaving... that made me fall on my knees for you. I don't want to lose you. I love you, and I'm so, so sorry."

In that moment, the weight of those five days disappeared. Everything we had gone through—the doubts, the silence, the almost-goodbye—it all dissolved into the words we shared in the quiet of the farewell. And for the first time in a long time, I felt like maybe, just maybe, we'd find our way through this together.

9
The last day at the gate

As i stood by the school gate, the memories of the last two years with Vivan rushed through my mind. The strictness of school had made our relationship complicated, but it also made every stolen moment even more precious. I remembered the mornings we catch a glimpse of each other—those few seconds that kept her going through the day.

Vivan stood in front of me, hands shoved in his pockets, looking equally worn out from the emotional weight of the day. I felt tears sting my eyes, but i forced them back, trying to keep myself together. It was the last time we'd seen each other for a while, and i wanted to be strong.

Me - softly, my voice trembling Remember those mornings when I'd be standing outside the class, just waiting to see you for a second before class started? Even those tiny moments felt like enough back then.

Vivan: nodding, smiling faintly "Yeah, I'd always time it just right, hoping you'd be there. And those quick glances—man, they kept me sane. It was like our own little secret in a world full of rules."

Maira: And those letters... Vivan, I still have every single one. Even though we couldn't talk much, passing those notes felt like such a lifeline.

Vivan's eyes softened, and he pulled out a crumpled piece of paper from his pocket, handing it to me.

Vivan: "I wrote you one more. I didn't know when I'd get a chance to give it to you, but... here.

I took the note, my fingers brushing against his, the warmth of the touch bittersweet.

Me: my voice breaking"I don't know how I'm going to get through the days without seeing you... even if it was just for a few minutes every morning."

Vivan steps closer, his eyes filled with the same pain she's trying to hide.

Vivan: we made it work, didn't we? Through the sneaking around, the letters, the early mornings... We survived two years of this madness, Maira. And we'll survive this too.

I looked down, my heart heavy with the thought of not seeing him. We have been through so much together—exchanging notes, sneaking glances, holding onto small moments in a strict environment that barely let us breathe together.

Me: whispering It just feels so different now, like this goodbye is too final.

Vivan sighs, stepping forward and gently wiping a tear from her cheek.

Vivan: "It's not the end. We've fought for this, for us, and that's not something that just ends. We'll find a way, like we always have."

I looked up at him, eyes filled with emotion, and suddenly, without thinking, i threw my arms around him, hugging him tightly. Vivan wraps his arms around me, holding me close as if trying to make the moment last forever.

Me: my voice muffled against his chest "I love you, Vivan. I just... I don't know when I'll see you again."

Vivan: whispering into my hair I love you too, Maira. More than you'll ever know. And no matter how far we are, I'll always be right here.

He pulls back slightly, placing her hand over his heart.

Vivan: Right here, okay? We'll meet again. I promise.

trying to hold onto that promise as we slowly let go of each other. Our hands linger, fingers brushing until we finally part, both knowing that this goodbye is temporary, but the ache feels permanent.

Me: smiling through my tears "Pata nahi kab milenge, but until then... I'll be waiting."

Vivan: smiling softly"Me too."

With one last look, we turn away, each carrying the weight of our memories and the hope of their next meeting...

I still don't understand how I fell in love with him so deeply, but once I did, there was no turning back. Our bond only grew stronger with each passing day—those late-night calls and the long paragraphs we sent to each other made everything feel more real, more meaningful.

One day, he casually told me, "I'm going on a 10-day trek, and I won't have my phone with me."

I paused, confused. "What? Who goes on a trek without a phone?"

But he assured me, explaining that his phone would be with his mom, so I shouldn't expect any messages for the next 10 days. It sounded strange, but I trusted him, so I didn't text him, not even once during those 10 days. It wasn't easy, but I kept reminding myself it was what he needed.

Then, on the 10th day, I saw his name pop up on my screen. Finally. I opened the message, only to find a long text.

"I didn't go on any trek. I lied. I had my CA Foundation exams, and I needed to focus on my studies. I couldn't tell you the truth, and I'm sorry for that."

I stared at the message, not knowing what to feel. A part of me was relieved that he was okay, but another part of me was hurt by the lie. Still, I understood why he did it. I took a deep breath and replied:

"It's okay. If you lied for your studies, then it's fine. I hope your exams went well."

He responded quickly, telling me that his exams had gone great, and a wave of relief washed over me. In that moment, the lie didn't seem to matter anymore. And He passed his exams, and that was enough for me. But before I let it go, I had to be honest with him.

"Vivan," I typed, "you could have told me the truth. I wouldn't have disturbed you, I promise. I understand how important your exams are. Just please don't lie to me next time. I promise, no matter what, I'll always understand."

His reply came almost instantly: "I'm sorry. I won't lie again. And with that, the weight of the lie was lifted. All that mattered was us, moving forward together, stronger than before.

10

Between love and Doubt

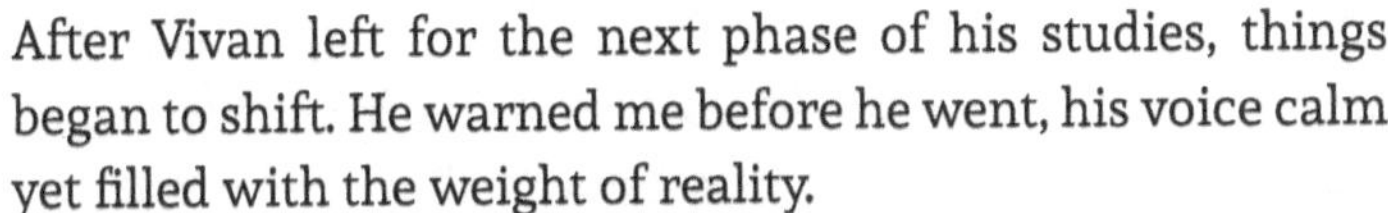

After Vivan left for the next phase of his studies, things began to shift. He warned me before he went, his voice calm yet filled with the weight of reality.

"I might not be able to give you as much time during this period," he said. "But you know I'm all yours, and you're all mine. Don't get distracted... We've made it this far, and we'll keep walking forward together."

I listened quietly, taking in his words. They felt heavy, but I knew deep down that he was right. Still, I couldn't let him think for even a second that I would let this distance weaken us. I took a deep breath before responding.

"I know, and I'm prepared for it," I said, trying to sound more confident than I felt. "And you, stupid, don't even think that just because you won't be able to give me enough time, I'll go looking for someone else! No... No one in this world could ever take your place. You're special... very special. I love you."

There was a pause on the other end, and I could almost feel him smile. "There's no chance of distraction for me, maira. I'll make you proud. I love you too. Be mine, forever."

"All yours," I whispered. "Not going anywhere."

That was the last deep conversation we had before things changed. I moved to Indore for my CAT preparation, living with my relatives. I took my studies seriously, especially since math wasn't my strongest subject. My classes were only two hours a day, but Vivan's stretched to eight or nine hours sometimes. I didn't want to disturb him during his preparation. I really wanted him to win in his own way, to grow without anything holding him back, including our relationship. That's what mattered to me most.

Our conversations became scarce. Sometimes we'd speak only two or three times a week, sometimes just once. Texts were even rarer, like sending letters through a crow and waiting for a reply. But whenever a reply came, the satisfaction was enough to keep us going. We were happy, even with the distance. I never doubted him—he was too serious about his studies to let anything get in the way.

But one day, while I was scrolling through Instagram, something made my heart sink. Vivan's ex had appeared on my feed again.and it showed him as a mutual friend. Frustration boiled inside me. I had already told him how much it hurt the last time this happened, and yet here we were again.

I couldn't hold it in. I texted him.

"Why did you follow her again? You know it bothers me." His reply came after a moment. "I'm sorry... I didn't really think about it, just did it. I won't do it again, promise."

I stared at the screen, feeling both angry and defeated. "Please, Vivan, don't do this. It really hurts me. I don't like it at all."

I was pissed, but I didn't make a big deal out of it. I didn't want to disturb him, I didn't want to cause him any stress that might affect his studies. So, I let it go. I told myself it didn't matter, that it was small, insignificant. But something had changed.

After that, I started stalking her—his ex. It became a habit, one I knew wasn't good for me, but I couldn't help it. And slowly, it started eating away at me.

After that, everything seemed to return to normal. For a few months, it felt like we were finally okay again—until that one evening. I was just mindlessly scrolling through Instagram when I stumbled upon a year-in-review post shared by one of our mutual friends. At first, it was just a harmless video, until that photo appeared.

It was Vivan. With her—his ex.

His hand rested on her shoulder, and they both looked so happy, like they had never been anything but the closest of friends. My heart dropped as I realized that this photo was from the day he left for another city. The same day he had said goodbye to me with promises of a future.

But the worst part wasn't even the photo—it was the fact that he hadn't told me. He never mentioned meeting her that day. I stared at the screen, unable to process what I was seeing. My chest felt like it was being crushed under the weight of betrayal, confusion, and heartbreak.

That night, I broke down. I cried until my body ached, begging God to show me a way out. I prayed, If he's not right for me, please take him away. I can't keep going through this. I felt utterly powerless.

The next day, I couldn't keep it inside anymore. The image of that photo haunted me, and I knew I had to confront him. My hands shook as I dialed his number, my heart racing with every ring.

"Hey," I whispered, barely able to speak.

"Hey, what's up?" he asked casually, as if nothing had changed.

I swallowed hard, trying to keep my voice steady. "I... I saw a photo yesterday. You and her. On Instagram, in a recap video. From the day you left."

There was a long pause. I could hear him breathe, but he said nothing at first. I could feel the silence pulling at my heart.

Finally, he spoke. "Look, it's not what you think. We just... ran into each other that day. It was nothing, really."

My heart clenched, the pain making it hard to breathe. "But why didn't you tell me? You never mentioned seeing her. You tell me everything, right? Why was your hand on her shoulder?"

His voice was too calm, too composed. "It was just a quick goodbye. A formality. She showed up, and we ran into each other accidentally. It didn't mean anything, I swear."

I wanted to scream, to tell him how much it hurt, how much it shattered me inside. But I was too broken to push any further. My heart still ached for the boy I loved.

"You're sure?" I asked, my voice barely holding together. "It didn't mean anything?"

"I'm sure," he said, his voice steady as ever. "You're the one I care about. Please, don't let this come between us. It was nothing."

I felt my walls crumble. Despite everything, I wanted so badly to believe him. I needed to believe him. He was everything I had, and I wasn't ready to lose that.

"Okay," I whispered, wiping away the tears that threatened to fall again. "I believe

And just like that, I forgave him.

I convinced myself that love was about giving second chances, about trusting someone even when it hurt. Maybe that's what love was supposed to be—blind faith in the person you couldn't imagine your life without.

"So we're good?" he asked softly, as if everything had already been fixed.

"Yeah," I said, my heart still heavy with pain, though my voice sounded lighter than it should have. "We're good."

And just like that, I let the hurt slip away. Again.

He always knew how to pull me back in. Every time, he'd find a way to make me believe, to make me stay, and like a fool, I'd give in. Every single time.

11

A year of waiting....and magical moments

It had been a year since we last saw each other, and my heart pounded with anticipation. Vivan had called to tell me he would be in Indore for a day, and it felt like everything might return to the way it used to be. I dressed carefully in the kurti and jeans he had suggested, my hands trembling slightly with a mix of nervousness and excitement. My mind raced—after all these months of long-distance, we would finally be together.

I walked into the mall, my eyes scanning the crowd as my phone buzzed in my hand. I quickly answered, my voice barely steady.

"Where are you?" I asked, almost breathless and millions of butterflies

"In front of Jack & Jones," he replied.

I spotted him, standing there with his back to me. My heart skipped a beat. Without thinking, I cut the call and ran towards him. The mall was bustling, but all I could see was him. My hand reached for his shoulder, the word catching in my throat before I could say it. "Vivan..." I whispered, almost afraid this was just a dream.

He turned immediately, and as his eyes met mine, everything else faded away. He pulled me into the tightest hug, and it felt like the world stopped. I could feel the months of longing dissolve in that one embrace. His scent, his warmth, everything felt so familiar, yet so different. He had changed, matured in the year apart, and yet, he was still the Vivan I knew. We stayed like that, staring at each other for what felt like forever, lost in a moment that neither of us wanted to end.

(He pulls away slightly, smiling.)
Vivan: I can't believe it's really you.
Me: (laughing softly) "I know... it feels unreal."

After a moment, he handed me a bouquet of flowers and some chocolates. "These are for you," he said, his voice softer, almost shy.

I smiled, my heart warming not because of the gifts but because of the thought behind them.

Me: "You didn't have to..."
Vivan: why? anything for you love

I was blushing

We decided to leave the mall before someone we knew saw us. As we hopped on his scooty, the familiar hum of the engine filled the air, but nothing felt ordinary about it. I leaned into him, pressing my weight against his back, my arms wrapped around him. The wind rushed past us as we rode in silence, but that silence spoke more than words ever could. I could feel the security of being close to him again after all this time.

The road emptied, and that's when Vivan broke the silence.

Vivan: "Did you watch Kabir Singh?"
Maira: (curious) "Yeah... why?"

He slowed the scooty, turning slightly to look at me, a mischievous grin on his face.

Vivan: "Remember the kiss on the bike?"

My face flushed as I realized where this was going, but I couldn't help but smile. "Yes..." I replied, my voice barely a whisper.

Vivan:"We could recreate that right now, you know?

My heart raced, but I nodded, unable to resist the moment. As we slowed down to a stop, I reached out and cupped his face, pulling him towards me. Our lips met for the first time in three and a half years, and it felt like magic. There was no rush, no urgency—just the feeling of finally closing the distance between us. When we pulled away, I felt a rush of shyness, but I held him even tighter, feeling both vulnerable and elated.

Me: (blushing) "That was... perfect."
Vivan: (smiling softly) "It was worth the wait."

We eventually reached the theater, but I couldn't tell you the name of the movie we watched. All I remember is holding his hand, sneaking kisses whenever we could, and feeling like every second with him made all those lonely nights bearable. The movie was just background noise—the real story was playing out between us.

Afterward, Vivan gave me news that made my heart leap. "I'm going to be in the city for a month," he said, his eyes twinkling with excitement.

Maira: "A month? Really?"
Vivan: "Yeah... we have time."

The next ten days were a blur of happiness. We spent as much time together as possible, exchanging small gifts, wandering through parks, and visiting temples. We even met each other's friends and family. But one moment in the temple stands out the most.

we were in temple, I asked him softly, "What did you pray for?"

He looked at me with a tender smile and replied, "I prayed that we always stay together. And if we can't... I asked God to keep us connected."

My heart swelled with emotion, and I smiled back. "We will always be together. There's no reason to think otherwise."

He nodded, pulling me close. "Yes, always."

But all good things have to end, and soon, the day arrived when he had to leave. We met at the park for one last time, both of us trying to make every moment count. He bought his bus ticket, and as we stood there, the reality of the situation hit me. My throat tightened, but I promised myself I wouldn't cry.

Me : (quietly) "Thank you for spending this time with me... I missed you so much before, but now, I think I'll miss you even more."

Vivan: (sighing, holding my hands) "Maira, I'm going to miss you more than you know. I love you. Don't give up on us—we've come this far, we'll go further together."

Me: "I love you more, and I won't give up on you. You mean the world to me. We'll meet again, right?"

Vivan:"Of course we will. Soon."

We hugged one last time, and I held onto him, not wanting to let go. It was the kind of hug that said everything we couldn't say in words. And then, he was gone. As I walked home, my heart ached with the loss, but I was also filled with gratitude—for the memories, for the love, for the chance to have experienced something so beautiful.

Weeks later, when I found out that Vivan had passed both groups of his Intermediate exams, I felt a swell of pride. All his sleepless nights, all the times he couldn't reply, all of it had been worth it. And for me, too—it was one of the best moments

12

The wounds That never heal

Everything between us had become stronger, more intense. But I didn't know that the perfect world I had built around us was about to shatter once again. It was just another day; I was casually scrolling through Instagram, when there it was—a familiar pain creeping back into my heart. He had followed her again. His ex. And this time, she followed him back. My fingers trembled as I stared at the screen, trying to piece together why this was happening again.

I thought about all the beautiful moments we had shared, the laughs, the endless conversations, the way he looked at me, as if I was the only person in the world. How could someone who cared so much repeat the very thing that tore me apart? In that moment, everything flooded back. Maybe it was me. Maybe I wasn't enough. Maybe I wasn't attractive enough, or successful enough. I picked myself apart, comparing every part of me to her. Why was he doing this again? Didn't he know how much this hurt me?

I stayed silent the entire day, unable to voice the storm brewing inside me. He noticed something was off, of course.

He always did.

"What's wrong?" He asked

"Nothing. We'll talk tonight," I replied, my words are colder than I intended. He didn't push further. But the weight of my silence lingered between us.

That night, he called. I couldn't hold it in anymore, so I finally asked. He explained it away, saying that when he had visited Indore, someone had asked him about crochet items, and he had mentioned her account. He said it so casually, as if it didn't matter.

"I told them about her because she makes crochet items. It was nothing."

"Are you her marketing team?" I shot back, my voice shaking with frustration. "Why did you follow her again? Why do you keep doing this?"

He sighed. "She has a boyfriend now, and I understand. I shouldn't have done it. I'm sorry."

I broke down. My voice cracked as I told him how much it hurt to see this happen again and again. "It boils my blood, Vivan. I can't handle it anymore. Why don't you understand?"

His voice softened. "Look, I haven't even talked to her much. Here, I'll show you." He sent me a screenshot of their last conversation on WhatsApp. In it, she had asked him, "Do you remember the song I liked the most?" He had replied, "How can you assume something so stupid?" And then she asked, "Are you not okay?"

It was brief, but the sting of it was enough.

I asked, "Why is her number still saved in your phone?"

He lied—right to my face. "It's not saved."

"Don't lie to me, Vivan," I said, my voice barely above a whisper. "It's right there. I can see it."

He paused, then finally admitted, "Okay, fine. I'll block and delete her. I promise I won't do this again. I'll never hurt you like this anymore."

wanted to believe him. I needed to believe him. But this time, I couldn't let it go so easily.

"If this happens again, Vivan, I'll leave. I won't be able to handle it anymore," I told him, my voice firm despite the ache in my chest. I knew his cousin's birthday was coming up, and his ex made crochet gifts. It was a connection I couldn't ignore.

"What are you giving Trisha for her birthday?" I asked, the dread already building up inside me.

"My dad already ordered a crochet bag from her," he replied, his tone nonchalant, as if he hadn't just crushed me all over again.

I couldn't believe it. "You're not going to pick it up, right?" I asked, holding onto the last thread of hope.

"No, I won't," he assured me.

I didn't know whether to trust him anymore. But how could I walk away after everything? After the memories we had made, after those ten perfect days together? Those couldn't have been a lie, could they? The way he looked at me, the love I saw in his eyes—it had to be real. It couldn't just vanish like this. So, I let it go. One more time. I forgave him because I wanted to believe that the love we shared was stronger than this. But deep down, I knew—some wounds never truly heal.

13

Echoes of insecurity

He made me believe in love again, or maybe I wanted to believe so badly that I convinced myself. I loved him too much to let go, even when insecurity crept in, slowly suffocating my peace of mind. I tried to erase everything from my memory—the doubts, the lies—but never once did I taunt him about it. I clung on because he was special, the kind of special that makes you feel leaving isn't an option, no matter how much it hurts.....in short i was obssesed with him.

Around the same time, a test happened at my coaching classes, and my results were far from what I had expected. I didn't get selected for the CAT+ batch, and I was devastated. I told him about it, hoping for comfort. And he did—he consoled me, telling me it was just the beginning and that I should work harder. He had his articleship at a big firm and was off on a trip with friends. Everything seemed smooth.

But deep down, I knew I needed to focus on my studies. This year was too crucial—I had been preparing for this exam for a year. The exam was set for November, and I couldn't afford any more distractions. So, I suggested we set fixed days to talk, like we did during his articleship. I needed to keep him out of my head all day so I could study. I wrote him a long message, suggesting we plan when to talk, and his reply was so...cold. "Thik hai, tere jaise marzi. Jo tujhe thik lage. Ya toh phir sirf Sunday ko baat karte hai."

I don't know why, but that message felt so rude. Why was he reacting like this? I asked him if something was wrong, if I had upset him, but he said nothing was wrong. I felt terrible, like I had done something wrong, and I dropped the plan. We decided to talk whenever, no rules, just as we had been. And for a week, things went back to normal.

Until one evening, his message popped up.

"I think you were right. We should take a break."

My heart sank. This morning, he'd sent me cute pictures of himself, and now, just hours later, he wanted a break. Confused and panicked, I texted him back: "What break? What do you mean?"

His reply shattered my heart: I've been wanting to tell you for a while. I talk to you every day because it's become routine, not because I want to."

His words felt like daggers. I tried to compose myself, barely managing to ask, "How long do you need? Will you come back?"

He didn't know. He didn't even know if he would ever come back.

And there I was, sitting alone in my hostel room, numb, trying to make sense of everything. I called him, desperate for answers, but he didn't pick up. I was spiraling, texting him long messages, apologizing, begging, hoping it was all a prank. But it wasn't. He was serious. The next day, I couldn't hold back anymore. I sent him a furious text, pouring out my frustration—how I was tired of asking for the bare minimum, how he was costing me my mental peace.

His reply the next day was unbelievable: "After reading your texts, I fainted in the metro. I'm already dealing with personal problems, and you're not helping."

Guilt washed over me. Again, I apologized, even though I didn't know what for. Then, out of sheer desperation, I called his older brother, asking if Vivan had mentioned fainting. His brother casually told me they had chatted for an hour on a video call the previous day, and Vivan seemed perfectly fine. My mind started spinning—was Vivan lying to me? But when he found out I had called his brother, he got upset, telling me I shouldn't have involved his family, that he didn't want them worrying about his health.

A few days later, he messaged me, "How's everything going?"

I wanted to lie and say, "I'm fine," but that wasn't the truth. So I told him the reality—how I wasn't eating, how I spent my days on my phone, distracting myself from everything, how I didn't think I could even pass the CAT exams anymore.

He apologized, saying, "Let's not do this. Let's fix everything." And for a moment, I was happy. I thought things were going to go back to normal, that he understood how badly this was affecting me. We started talking again, but it wasn't the same.

I finally asked him, "Is something wrong? Are you struggling?"

He hesitated before saying, "Yes, there's a problem."

Trying to be mature, I replied, "That's okay. Focus on your studies and your career. Relationships can wait."

He thanked me for understanding, but deep down, I wasn't sure if I truly did.

One thing that's really bothering me is why he never thought about how much of an overthinker I am or how important this year is for me. Knowing that this breakup could ruin my dreams, I can't help but wonder why he didn't care about my feelings. Was it all just a way to pass the time for him?

Did he find someone else at work? That thought brings so much self-doubt—making me feel like I'm not good enough, like I'm not doing well in life, and like I'm missing out on everything. This self-doubt hit me hard, leaving me feeling lost and unworthy.

14
A Broken Goodbye

I couldn't believe it. The pain of losing him transformed into something more—an ache so deep, it became physical. I dialed his number, but he didn't pick up; he was at work. Later, as I sat before a plate of rice I couldn't bring myself to eat, he called back. I picked up the phone, sobbing, "Vivan, I can't do this. I can't move on... I can't even study anymore, I'm lost."

He was gentle but firm, "Dheere dheere, sab theek ho jayega... sab theek ho jayega." He was trying to calm me down, but my desperation spilled over. "Please don't go, I can't handle this—please."

He sighed, "Yaar, you're making this harder for both of us. If it's too much, talk to your friends, get support. You'll be okay."

The call ended, and so did my composure. I vomited the few spoonfuls of rice I had managed. That day, I realized how helpless I was, how far I'd fallen from the dreams I once had. My dream of cracking CAT, gone—because I loved him so much, too much to let go easily.

I packed my things and left for home, hoping the familiar comfort would dull the pain. Days passed in a blur of overthinking until Vivan called again. "How are you?" he asked, his voice soft, as if he already knew the answer.

"I'm at home," I said. "Maybe I'll be okay... someday."

His next words hurt more than I expected. "We had such a good bond—can't we still be friends?"

I forced a smile through my tears. "How can I be just your friend, after imagining my whole life with you? After loving you, after all the kisses, the dreams... Is that even possible?"

He hesitated, then said, "It's not easy for me either. Who knows, maybe one day we'll come back together after sorting out our lives. Maybe it's just a matter of time..."

In my loneliness, I agreed. I thought maybe staying in touch was better than nothing at all. But I was wrong—so wrong. The very next day, I found out he had followed his ex again on Instagram, and she followed him back.

My heart shattered. I texted him, furious: Is this why we broke up? I hate you! You're obsessed with her!

He replied, denying everything: I'm not obsessed with her. I was just trying to normalize myself. You don't understand!

My reply was cold and final: Marry her, Vivan. Or get over her. Because if you don't, whoever is with you next will suffer, just like I did.

After a few more texts, he asked me to stop, but I couldn't. My heart was too broken. Finally, I said, No more contact. I can't pretend to be your friend when I'll always love you.

For a while, there was silence. But then he texted again, and this time he opened up about the family issues he had never shared with me before—and, his mother's health, the stress that had weighed him down. I felt a pang of guilt. I had overreacted, thinking everything was about me, when he had been dealing with things I couldn't even imagine.

We had one last emotional conversation. He gave me hope again, that maybe things could be okay. But before long, that hope crumbled when he suddenly canceled our plans to meet because his parents were visiting. My heart sank as I texted him one last time: Can we sort things out? Or should I just move on?

His reply was simple yet devastating: We've hurt each other too much. It's better we stay a part of each other's lives but not become life. This isn't what I wanted, but it's how it is.

I stared at the message, feeling the finality in it. It wasn't just a breakup—it was closure, the kind that crushes your soul but also sets you free. I texted back: Thank you for this closure. I didn't want it, but now I'm clear.

Then he came back into my life after all the closure, asking me, "Can't you love someone without expecting a relationship?" I couldn't help but laugh. I was already doing that, and trust me, it tears you apart from the inside. Loving someone, knowing they can't be yours, hurts so much. He wasn't a part of my life anymore, but he also wasn't completely gone, and that confusion was killing me. Ugh, the uncertainty of whether we were together or not never left my mind. Whenever he reached out, I always answered his calls, and that was my mistake. I should have stuck to no contact; maybe I would have moved on faster.

After that, we started following each other on Twitter. He saw some of my tweets that he found hurtful. One of them read: "The biggest fear of girls is building a man for another woman." He taunted me about it, and I explained, "That's not how I feel. I just posted it to get good reach."

Then, not long after, he changed his header photo to one where he was tying the shoelaces of some girl. My heart raced like it was about to explode. I called him immediately, asking how he could move on so quickly. He clarified that he was helping her because her hand was injured. So, I asked, "Then what's the point of posting it on social media?" He replied, "Just like you said you post things on Twitter for good reach, I did the same." That was it for me; I blocked him right then, and he blocked me too.

After that, my account got suspended. When I created a new one, we somehow connected again. This time, I tweeted, "Why can't you people sleep?" One of my Twitter friends replied, "Can't say." I replied, "Oh, you just came from the office?" He answered, "Yeah! Just at 9 PM." I joked, "Why do you even come home? Just sleep in the office!"

He read our conversation, and I don't know what hurt him so much, but he ended up blocking me everywhere.
Why did he block me? Why did it all go wrong when we still cared for each other so much?
It all began with a text—a simple SMS, the only way I could reach him after he had blocked me everywhere else. I had asked him, with trembling hands, why he had done it. I didn't expect much from him anymore, but even then, his reply shook me to the core.
"I'm already in such a vulnerable position," he had said. "I've been trying to move on. I don't know how difficult it is for you, but it's horrifying for me. Yesterday, I saw you talking to this guy on Twitter, that CA finalist guy—and the way you were talking to him... it was the way you used to talk to me. It got on my nerves. I can't take it anymore. I've been trying to stay calm, to focus on my studies, but I keep thinking about you. Seeing things like that... it breaks me. I asked for us to separate so we could both focus, but being in touch like this isn't working for either of us."
He was jealous. That simple, normal interaction I had with another guy was enough to push him over the edge. I could

feel his frustration, his pain, through his words, and I knew then that our separation was tearing him apart just as much as it was breaking me.

I sat there with his words echoing in my mind, and all I could think about was how similar we were in our suffering, yet so far apart in how we dealt with it. I replied, pouring my heart into a message that I knew he might never answer.

"No one in this world can ever take your place, Vivan. I know exactly how you feel because I've been there too. I've blocked you before, too, remember? I did it because I knew that if I saw anything, it would drive me crazy. It's not easy for either of us. But if blocking me helps you, then go for it. I want you to be the same Vivan I knew—the one I fell in love with. Maybe we need each other the most right now, and yet we're both trying to get away from each other. I don't know. All I know is that I love you... and I always will. Take care."

I waited. And waited.

But the silence was deafening. It became clear that this was the end of our story—the end I never wanted but had to accept.

I started to wonder. Is this really what I deserve after everything I gave to him? After all the love, the patience, the support? Was this how it was supposed to end, with no closure, no final words, just a painful silence?

I always knew life had its own problems, but what hurt the most was that he never discussed those problems with me. He shut me out, and the distance between us only made things worse. But that wasn't the only thing that tore us apart. There was always something else lingering in the background—something that made me doubt our story from the beginning.

It was his ex. Even after knowing how much it hurt me, he

stayed in contact with her, lying to me, thinking I would never find out. But I did. And the moment I realized he was willing to lie, willing to hurt me in that way, I knew something had changed. That was the day I blocked him. Not out of anger, but out of a desperate need to protect myself from the life he was offering me—a life I couldn't accept.

Because no matter how much I loved him, I couldn't pretend anymore. I couldn't entertain the idea of a future with someone who wasn't willing to change for me, who wasn't afraid of losing me. He was a good guy, sure. Handsome, intelligent, the kind of person any girl would want to build a life with. But I realized he would never be that person for me.

He would make an amazing husband one day, a great father even. But not with me. And that was okay. I had to let go of the idea that he was the one for me because deep down, I knew he wasn't.

It hurt. God, it hurt more than anything I had ever felt. But at the same time, there was a strange sense of peace that came with it. I had tried—tried everything I could to bring him back, to make it work. But it wasn't enough. Sometimes, love isn't enough.

I closed my eyes and took a deep breath, letting the tears fall as I whispered to myself, "This is what it's meant to be." If we weren't meant to work out, it wasn't for a lack of trying. It was because life had other plans for us, plans we couldn't see coming.

I realized then that I didn't fear losing him anymore. I had already lost him. And maybe that was for the best.

Vivan would go on to live his life, and I would live mine. He would find someone else—someone who would be better for him, and I would find my own path. It was a bittersweet ending, but it was our ending.

I had loved him with all my heart, and he had loved me in his own way. But sometimes, love stories don't have happy endings. And that's okay.

The biggest lesson I've learned is that forgiveness should mean something. You can forgive someone two or three times, but when you keep forgiving them for the same hurt over and over, six or seven times? That's when you lose yourself. If they don't care enough to understand what hurts you or what makes you feel small, then you will never be happy with them, no matter how much you love them.

We often think, What will happen if I lose them? Will I ever be able to move on? How will I survive without them? These thoughts haunt you, making you feel like your world will fall apart if they're gone. But the truth is, if someone doesn't want to stay, if they don't want to understand your pain, no matter how many times you try to explain, then even if they come back after every fight, you'll always be the one adjusting. You'll always be the one bending just to keep them from leaving. And that's not fair, is it?

Life doesn't end just because one person leaves. It feels like it does, but it doesn't. There's so much more to life than this heartbreak. So much more than just love from one person. It took me a long time to realize that, but now I know. Life has so much to offer beyond the pain and beyond that one person who couldn't see your worth. You are more than enough, and there's a whole world waiting for you outside of that hurt.

Sometimes, we hold on so tightly because we're afraid of the unknown, but what we don't realize is that letting go can be the first step toward finding peace, toward finding yourself again. Yes, love is beautiful, but so is living for yourself, so is finding happiness in your own heart. There's so much more to life than the love we thought we couldn't live without. There's a whole future waiting, and it's time to embrace it.

As long as your happiness depends on someone else, you'll never truly be happy. Start feeling sufficient within yourself, and life will get better.

This was the end of maira and vivan love story—a story that taught me about love, about loss, and about letting go.